D1068841

Seth Odom

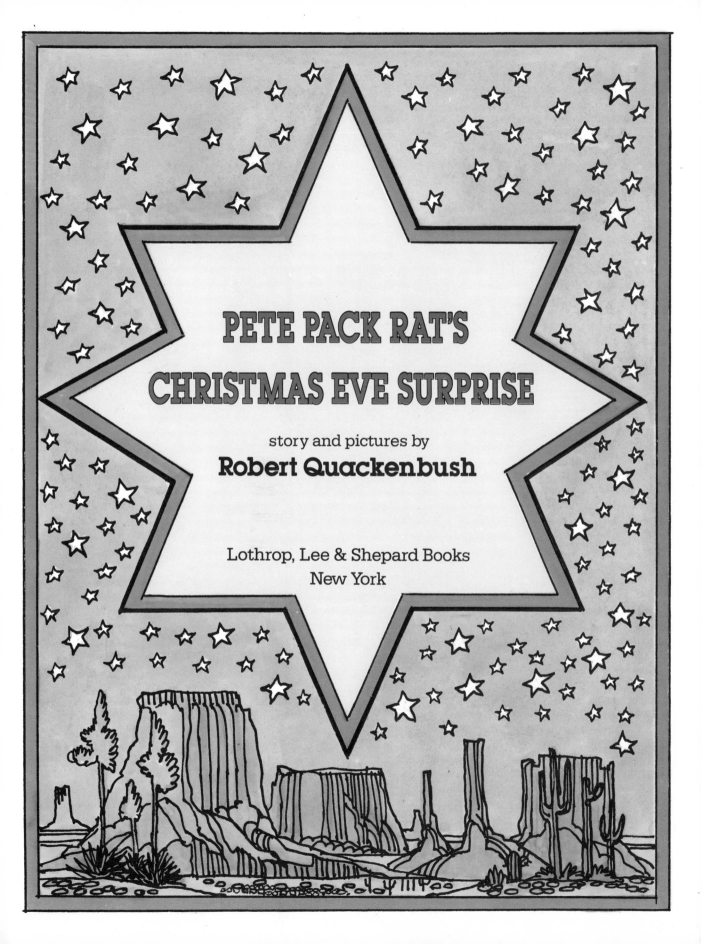

PETE PACK RAT'S
CHRISTMAS EVE SURPRISE

story and pictures by
Robert Quackenbush

Lothrop, Lee & Shepard Books
New York

For Piet

Copyright © 1981 by Robert Quackenbush. All rights reserved. No part of this book may be reproduced or utilized in any form or by any means, electronic or mechanical, including photocopying, recording or by any information storage and retrieval system, without permission in writing from the Publisher. Inquiries should be addressed to Lothrop, Lee & Shepard Books, a division of William Morrow & Company, Inc., 105 Madison Avenue, New York, New York 10016. Printed in the United States of America. First Edition.
1 2 3 4 5 6 7 8 9 10

Library of Congress Cataloging in Publication Data
Quackenbush, Robert M.   Pete Pack Rat's Christmas Eve surprise.
Summary: Pete Pack Rat prevents the Gila Monster Gang from ruining Pebble Junction's Christmas celebration. [1. West (U.S.)—Fiction. 2. Animals—Fiction. 3. Christmas stories] I. Title.
PZ7.Q16Pg   [E]   81-1908
ISBN 0-688-00630-2   AACR2   ISBN 0-688-00631-0 (lib. bdg.)

Christmas Eve was only a few hours away. Everyone in Pebble Junction was excited about the holiday. First they would all march in a parade down Main Street. Then they would fill the dance hall to see a Christmas play. After the play there would be a party onstage and a piñata would be broken. Presents would fall to the floor for everyone!

The Gila Monster Gang was locked safely in jail and there were no other outlaws on the prowl. There was no need to worry that anyone would ruin their celebrations. Or so they thought.

Pete Pack Rat was in charge of making the piñata. He had been working on it for days. He started with a clay pot and some wire coathangers. He covered the pot and the wire frame with bits of pasted-down tissue paper. When it was just the way he wanted it, he stuffed it with the presents everyone had dropped by earlier, and sat down to wait. Sheriff Sally Gopher had promised to send her wagon to deliver the piñata safely to the dance hall.

At last, Pete heard the sound of a wagon outside. He opened his door and saw the sheriff's wagon, but he almost didn't recognize it because it was fixed up to look like Santa's sleigh. In the driver's seat sat Summers and Winters Jackrabbit, the sheriff's deputies, wearing Santa Claus suits. Pulling the wagon was the sheriff's horse, Jake, dressed as one of Santa's reindeer.

"What a float!" cried Pete. "But whoever heard of twin Santa Clauses?"

"Shucks," said Summers. "I'm Santa Claus from the North Pole."

"And I'm Santa Claus from the South Pole," said Winters.

"That's the first I've heard of that," said Pete. "Well, let's get the piñata on board."

Summers and Winters and Pete loaded the piñata on the wagon, climbed aboard, and headed down the road to the dance hall.

On the way, they passed the jailhouse. The Gila Monster Gang looked out from their barred window at the piñata going by and their mouths drooled. But they pretended that they weren't interested.

"Phooey on Christmas!" they hollered.

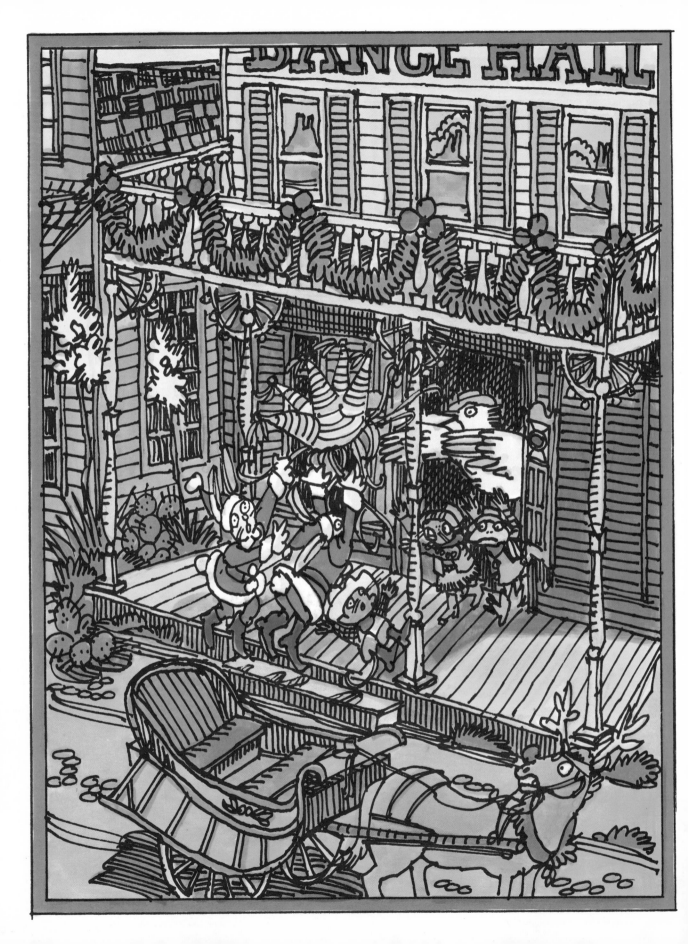

The wagon pulled up in front of the dance hall. Sheriff Sally Gopher and her other two deputies, Rosa Roadrunner and Gracie Gecko, came running when they heard it. They got there just in time to see Pete and the twins trip on a step and almost drop the piñata. The sheriff and Rosa and Gracie grabbed it just as it was about to come crashing to the ground.

"Whew!" said Pete. "We almost had an early Christmas Eve!"

"Let's take the piñata inside and hang it before anything else happens," said Sheriff Sally. "You did a beautiful job, Pete."

"I'm glad you like it, Sally," said Pete. "I had a few problems making it before I got it right, but I'll tell you about that some other time. Lead the way for us so we don't trip again."

Inside the dance hall, the twins got a stepladder and hung the piñata above the center of the stage. Then they all stood back to admire it.

"Wonderful!" said Sheriff Sally. "It looks just like a Christmas star. Now everything is done. Let's straighten up and get ready for the parade."

They put away the ladder and went around the hall picking up scraps and arranging chairs.

Suddenly there was a lot of commotion, and Jake Horse burst into the hall, wagon and all.

"Jake!" cried the sheriff. "Have you gone loco?"

"Quick, Sheriff!" cried Jake. "There's been a jailbreak!"

"The Gila Monster Gang!" everyone gasped.

When they got to the jailhouse, half of the town
was already there. Sheriff Sally Gopher's father, the
jailkeeper, was sitting at his desk looking dazed.

"Pop! What happened?" cried Sheriff Sally.

"Something terrible, Sally," answered Sam Gopher.
"I sat down awhile ago to rest my feet. I must have
dozed off, because the next thing I knew the Gang was
escaping."

"But it was impossible for them to escape," said the
sheriff. "There was a special lock on their cell."

"I know," said Sam Gopher. "But I was careless and
left a broom by the cell door. They must have used it as
a hook to get the key to their cell from the keyboard.
Then they unlocked the door, knocked me down, and
tore out of the jailhouse before I could stop them."

"Which way did they go, Pop?" asked Sheriff Sally.

"They went that-a-way," he answered, pointing across the desert. "They rode off on their old horse that's been serving time in the corral behind the jailhouse."

"Well," said Sheriff Sally, "five crooks on one crooked horse won't get very far. My deputies and I can round them up in a jiffy tomorrow."

She turned to Pete and the twins.

"Go light the candles for the Christmas lights and get the wagon in position for the parade," she said.

Then she turned to the rest of the crowd.

"All of you go home and get dressed for the parade," she said. "Everything begins in an hour, as planned."

"Yippee!" they all shouted.

Everyone followed Sally Gopher's orders, except Pete
Pack Rat, Jake Horse, and the Jackrabbit twins, who
kept going up and down the street in the wagon.

Sheriff Sally Gopher's window opened as they were
making one last trip. She called out, "What are you
fellows doing? Why aren't you lighting the candles? It
will be dark soon and we'll have no Christmas lights."

"Right away, Sally," Pete called back. "We just had a
few things to do first."

Sheriff Sally shook her head in puzzlement and closed
her window.

"Shouldn't we tell the sheriff what we have been
doing?" asked Jake.

"Later," answered Pete. "Anyway, we're finished now,
so let's light the candles as Sally asked."

The candles had been put in the sand-filled paper bags and placed atop roofs and along the streets. Soon Pebble Junction was aglow with hundreds of Christmas lights.

"YAAAHOOOO!" cried the twins with their loudest rebel yell.

Now the festivities could begin!

Everyone in town heard them and came running to take their places in the parade. Pete Pack Rat blew a whistle and the band began to play. The sheriff's wagon rolled down the street and everyone began marching behind it.

"MERRY CHRISTMAS! HO! HO! HO!" shouted the twins as loud as they could over the blaring trumpets, crashing cymbals, and pounding drums.

Everyone cheered with joy.

Suddenly, an old horse came from nowhere and plowed right into the parade. Everyone was knocked to the ground and the wagon was tipped over. It was the Gila Monster Gang!

"Stop them!" cried the sheriff.

But it all happened so fast, no one knew what to do. Everyone watched in horror as the Gang galloped down the street and stormed into the dance hall. Before anyone could move, the Gang came out again and disappeared into the night.

"Our piñata!" cried the sheriff. "The Gila Monsters have stolen our piñata! All of our presents are inside it!"

The crowd was furious. There was much shouting
and yelling and crying.

Pete Pack Rat ran over to the sheriff and said, "Sally, I
must tell you something. I—"

"Not now, Pete," interrupted Sheriff Sally. "Can't you
see I must calm this crowd?"

She ordered her deputies to turn her wagon upright.
Then she jumped up on it and took command.

"Settle down, folks," she ordered. "I'll not let those
crooks ruin our Christmas Eve."

"But what about our piñata?" someone cried.

"Don't worry about it," answered Sheriff Sally. "My
deputies and I will get it back tomorrow when we arrest
the Gang. You will all have your presents on Christmas
Day instead of tonight, that's all. So let's get on with the
parade and the other festivities!"

The band began playing again and the parade went on. Soon everyone was back in the holiday spirit. They marched down the street to the dance hall and then went inside to see the play.

"Where's Pete?" Sheriff Sally asked Rosa Roadrunner.

"I saw him leave with Jake and the twins," answered Rosa.

"That's strange," said Sheriff Sally. "Why would Pete leave now?"

Inside the hall, Sheriff Sally kept looking around for Pete. Was he too heartbroken about the stolen piñata to come to the play? Was that what he wanted to tell her?

The curtain went up and Hattie Squirrel came on the stage. She told the story of the first Christmas and how the gentle animals came to the manger. Then she sang:

> There was a donkey standing by,
> Christmas Day, Christmas Day.
> There was a donkey standing by,
> Christmas Day in the morning.

As Hattie sang, Doug Donkey stepped out on the stage and sang with her. Then Hattie sang verses about each of the other gentle animals that had come to the manger that night so long ago. Elly Cow, Morris Ram, Mandy Goat, and Tilly Dove joined them on cue and sang along.

Sheriff Sally leaned over to the row of chairs in front of her and whispered to Rosa Roadrunner, "It would all be so perfect if only Pete's beautiful piñata was hanging over the manger."

And at that moment Pete, Jake Horse, and the Jackrabbit twins came into the dance hall, singing along at the top of their voices. They were carrying something, but it was hard to see what it was because everyone had stood up to have a look.

"What is happening?" cried the sheriff.

Pete, Jake, and the twins climbed up on the steps. They were carrying the Christmas piñata!

They hung the piñata back in place and the audience cheered wildly. Then the play ended and everyone rushed onstage. Sheriff Sally made her way through the crowd.

"Pete!" she cried. "How...? Where...?"

"Easy, Sally," answered Pete. "There were two piñatas. Remember how I said that I had a few problems making it? Well, first I made one that turned out to be too small for all the presents. So I had to make a new one. When I heard about the jailbreak, I switched the piñata with our presents in it for the little one, with the help of Jake and the twins. I knew the Gila Monster Gang would want our presents."

"So *that's* what you were doing with the wagon," said Sheriff Sally. "But where did you put the real piñata?"

"In the safest place of all," answered Pete. "The jailhouse!"

"You mean the Gang stole an empty piñata?" asked Sheriff Sally.

"Not exactly," answered Pete. "I filled it with a few surprises, like chocolate-covered soap. I think we can expect a quick return from the Gang after they have sampled some of my surprises for them."

And he was right! No sooner had he spoken than the Gang came bursting into the hall with soap bubbles pouring out of their mouths.

"Help! Help! We're dying!" they cried. "Get us a doctor!"

Everyone roared with laughter.

"You'll live, boys," said Sheriff Sally. "Take them back to jail, deputies."

She picked up a plum pudding from the party table and handed it to one of the deputies.

"Take this along for the Gang's Christmas supper," she said.

"MERRY CHRISTMAS TO EVERYONE!" cried Pete Pack Rat.

"HO! HO! HO!" finished the twins. With that, the party began. Everyone stuffed themselves with cactus candy, star cookies, and punch. Then Sheriff Sally blindfolded Pete and he swung a long, wooden pole and broke the piñata. Everyone scrambled for the presents that came falling to the ground. There were toy soldiers and dolls for the children, and gold rings, bracelets, and watches for the grown-ups.

And so, thanks to Pete Pack Rat and his talent for tricking outlaws, Pebble Junction had the best Christmas Eve anyone there could remember.

About the Author

Robert Quackenbush has illustrated over one hundred books, nearly half of which he has also written. His works include picture books, song books, fiction, nonfiction, and easy readers, such as his well-loved Detective Mole series. His books have received awards and citations from AIGA and the Society of Illustrators, and his graphics have been exhibited in leading museums in this country. Mr. Quackenbush lives in New York City with his wife, Margery, a fashion designer and teacher, and their son, Piet.

This is the third adventure for Pete Pack Rat, following *Pete Pack Rat* and *Pete Pack Rat and the Gila Monster Gang.* Pete also appears in *Sheriff Sally Gopher and the Haunted Dance Hall.*